# Sun Moon Daughter

BY DAVID D. FIX AND STEVEN G. HAMMING, PSYD

HEARTH PRODUCTIONS LLC
GRAND RAPIDS, MICHIGAN

Photo credit: Amelia Falk

David is a teacher, author and artist interested in empowering others. Having seen how divorce can hurt the children involved, he was inspired to create *Sun Moon Daughter* as a way to give children their power back in a seemingly powerless situation.

*He would like to thank his beautiful wife Nicole, Bob and Phyllis Fix, Robert Fix, James and Joelle Fix, Lon Lefanty, Larry and Kathy Johnston, Jim and Lisa Haughey, Maria Rodriguez, Ralph Stadelman, Doug Jantz, Marialyce Zeerip, Doug Kleyn, Dr. Hamming, Elizabeth Kennedy, Tyler Bedgood, Denise Iwaniw, Joe Cherian, and many others.*

www.HearthProductions.com

Photo credit: Joseph Petz

Dr. Hamming is a psychologist, collaborative divorce coach, and father of five who has had to walk his own children through the storm of a difficult divorce. Taking from both his clinical and personal experience, he seeks to assist other families in their time of reorganization. He is also a member of the International Academy of Collaborative Professionals.

*He would like to thank his amazing wife, Pam, for her undying love, support, and teamwork, for assisting him while they helped their children adjust to their changing family life. A big thanks to his five wonderful children who have demonstrated resilience and hope throughout the journey.*

www.DrSteveHamming.com

Hearth Productions LLC

Library of Congress control number: 2012922554    ISBN: 978-0-9886851-1-6

Printed by Grandville Printing Company. Grand Rapids, Michigan. First printing, February 2013.

# FOREWORD

Dear Concerned Reader,

Because you have chosen this book you likely have a child in your life trying to cope with the difficult reality of divorce. This book was written with the hope of helping children understand the very adult decision to end a marriage.

Divorce is usually a very complicated, messy ordeal that barely makes sense to the adults involved and almost always is very confusing for the children who have to sort out this unsolicited change in their lives. Although divorce is a common experience these days, in the life of a child it might still be a mystery - and an often difficult one to assimilate into his or her young understanding of how life works.

To make the greatest use of this book, simply read it through the first time with your child. Once acquainted with the story, please read it to your child again and utilize the divorce themes found at the back of the book. These are universal themes that often occur in both the parent's and the child's experience during a divorce.

The theme questions are designed to help solicit your child's private thoughts and feelings about what he or she is going through. This might give you a greater insight into your child's inner life and thus assist you to connect more deeply with him or her.

Finally, this book was written to inspire hope. The story concludes with Grace finding a way to move forward. She discovers the crucial ability to create separate and meaningful relationships with each of her parents. Divorce changes lives, but possibilities for meaning and love still remain.

Steven G. Hamming, PsyD

In a starry sky, the Sun and the Moon met and fell in love. The kisses the Moon blew to the Sun caught fire in licks of flame. One fiery kiss burned across the heavens and fell from the sky, striking a tree and landing deep in the Earth.

The tree grew a hollow where it had been struck and mended its wound with soot and bark. And where the fiery kiss had been buried, something began to grow. The Sun and Moon watched carefully as their child grew from the ground, sprouting from the Earth. They named their heavenly daughter Grace. And they loved her.

Grace grew up in the field by the hollow tree and the reflecting pool. Her parents were always near, holding her with warmth and light. Whenever Grace would look down into the pool, she would see her own reflection with the Sun and Moon looking over her shoulders. She saw three smiling faces looking up from the surface of the water.

Grace would gather different colored leaves and place them on the ground to create a picture of her family. Grace used orange leaves for the Sun, yellow for the Moon and red for herself. The Sun and Moon enjoyed seeing the leaf pictures of their family.

Grace would also play in the shadows created by the Sun and Moon's light shining through the hollow tree's branches. After playing with the Sun and Moon, Grace would lie down for a nap in the hollow of the tree while her parents watched over her.

One day, during her nap, a loud storm startled Grace. Darkness rolled overhead, and a strong wind blew. The leaf pictures of her family were getting all mixed up. Even her reflection in the pool became upset.

Grace ran around and around trying to keep her leaves from blowing away, but the storm was too strong. Grace looked up and saw that the Sun and Moon were not looking over her anymore. Now they were getting in each other's way. The sky grew dark as the Sun and Moon fought.

Grace yelled to her parents in the sky, "Stop fighting!" But the Sun and Moon didn't notice her. Rain fell and the wind blew. Grace ran into the hollow of the tree, and it lowered its branches to shelter her. Tears fell like the rain on her face. As the Sun slid behind the Moon, Grace closed her eyes and did not open them for a long time.

When Grace finally peeked out, the Sun and Moon were far away and the sky was dim. Their fighting had scattered her leaves across the field farther than she could see. Grace began to pick them up one at a time. She followed the trail of leaves a long distance.

When she had gathered up the last one, Grace found herself in a dark, strange forest. She could barely see her hand in front of her face. She looked around and cried out, "Is anyone out there?" The eerie sounds of the woods were the only thing she heard. Grace felt lost and alone.

A little way off, Grace saw green lights dancing through the forest. As the lights came closer, she saw they were lightning bugs! The lightning bugs swarmed around her, lighting up the forest with a green glow. Grace looked down. She was able to see her footprints and followed them out of the forest.

Grace thanked the lightning bugs at the forest's edge and continued on her way. She walked for a long time, retracing her steps. Finally, she saw the hollow tree far off in the distance and ran to it.

Grace was very happy to be back home. She put her leaves on the ground and tried to remake the picture of her family. But when she leaned over the pool and looked into the water, behind her reflection was only an empty sky. Where there used to be three faces, now there was just hers.

Grace asked the hollow tree, "Why aren't the Sun and Moon watching over me right now? I don't like it when they fight, and I don't like it when we're not all together either."

The hollow tree and Grace looked into the pool and saw only their reflections. The hollow tree said, "I don't know where the Sun and Moon are right now, and I don't know when all of you will be back together again."

In the distance, the Sun appeared. It wandered across the sky with warmth and light, searching for Grace. Grace felt excited to see the Sun again, but the Moon wasn't there. And the Sun didn't seem as playful. Confused, Grace stayed silent. She hid behind the hollow tree and moved with the shadows as the Sun passed overhead. The Sun kept wandering, moving over the sky and out of sight.

Then the Moon appeared on the edge of the sky. The Moon was looking for Grace too. Feeling unsure about what was happening between her parents, Grace stayed hidden in the shadows. She watched the Moon cross the sky and disappear over the horizon.

Feeling alone, Grace leaned over the pool. A tear ran down her face and dropped into the water. The drop created a ripple that spread across the pool. Grace knelt down and touched the water. She watched the ring she created spread across the pool too.

Again the Sun rose. The Sun shone down, reaching for Grace with her love. Less afraid, Grace stepped into the Sun's light and her eyes sparkled. She enjoyed being held in the Sun's warmth once again.

As the Sun began to set, the Moon rose. When the Moon passed overhead, Grace saw herself glowing in the Moon's color. It made her look more grown-up. She liked her reflection in the Moon's light and the feeling of being safe.

Grace smiled as she imagined a new way to relate to each of her parents. She began gathering feathers and stones from the field and placing them beside the reflecting pool.

When the Sun appeared again, Grace placed the feathers in the pool and looked at the reflection in the water. On the surface of the water, the feathers appeared like clouds in the sky. Grace saw herself smile and felt the Sun shining over her shoulders once again.

She stood up and called to the Sun, "Look what I made just for you! Do you like my present?" The Sun was happy to see Grace playing again and loved the feather clouds floating in the pool. Grace played in the Sun's light, moving the feathers around on the surface of the water. The Sun shone down on Grace and she felt warm and happy.

As the Sun moved across the sky and out of sight, the Moon rose. Grace took the stones she had gathered from the field and placed them into the pool. As the Moon moved overhead, it gently pulled the water away from the edges, revealing wet stones that sparkled like stars in the night sky.

She called to the Moon, "Look at the present I made just for you!" The Moon was happy to see her and loved the shiny star stones. Grace played in the Moon's glow, shifting the stones to create new patterns. The Moon shone down on Grace and she felt safe and peaceful.

As the Moon continued across the sky and began to disappear, the Sun slowly came back again. Grace asked the hollow tree, "Whose fault is it that the Sun and Moon are apart? Is it mine?"

The hollow tree answered, "You are certainly not to blame."

"Will they ever share the same sky again?" Grace wondered.

The hollow tree said, "I'm not sure."

Each day the Sun rose into the sky and watched over Grace as she made feather clouds in the reflecting pool. Each night the Moon rose and watched over Grace as she made star patterns with shiny stones. Once in a while the Sun and Moon would meet in the sky and spend time together, but usually they stayed in their separate spaces...and Grace loved them both.

## BEGINNINGS

<u>Parent</u>: It might be difficult to reflect on the positive beginning of your relationship as it may deepen the pain of your current loss. However, it will help your child to hear you speak in a balanced way about your relationship story.

<u>Child</u>: Your parents had a loving beginning to which you were invited. Be assured that the start of your lives together as a family was one of celebration.

Why do you think the Moon blew kisses to the Sun?
How do you think the Sun felt about being kissed?

## ROUTINES

<u>Parent</u>: Children have assumptions about life based on their experiences. Anything that challenges their assumptions can cause anxiety. Try to hear your child's assumptions about how he or she understands life.

<u>Child</u>: Your family, too, has activities, routines and traditions that are very important. They give you a sense of how your family works and what is valuable to all of you.

How do you imagine Grace felt inside while she was playing with the Sun and Moon?
How did the Sun and Moon show Grace that they loved her?

## DISRUPTION

<u>Parent</u>: Children experience divorce like a powerful storm that rearranges their world. The real reason children attempt to get their parents back together is because they want their world back, not because they believe in the health of their parent's relationship. Losing the orderliness of their lives is more disruptive than you might realize.

<u>Child</u>: Children will try to make sense of their parent's fighting, but usually cannot. This is a time to trust your parent's thinking and believe that they are looking out for you.

What do you think Grace is feeling now?
What were the Sun and Moon fighting about?

## POWERLESSNESS

<u>Parent</u>: Divorce leaves children feeling powerless. It will be helpful to recognize that it is necessary for your children to feel powerful and heard in some way about what is going on around them. Find opportunities to give them choices.

<u>Child</u>: Your parents probably won't change their minds and do what you want. This does not mean that they are not listening, nor does it mean that they don't care about you.

What would you have said to Grace as she was hiding inside the hollow of the tree?
How do you think Grace felt when the Sun and the Moon weren't paying attention to her?

## REORGANIZE

<u>Parent</u>: Children feel lost and confused about what is going on during a divorce. They organize as a way to manage their feelings. Recognize this organizing as fear, and encourage your child to voice his or her feelings out loud.

<u>Child</u>: Having fears causes children to pull away from others and become quiet. However, it is more helpful to talk about your fears and questions with someone who you really trust.

How is Grace trying to help herself?
What do you think Grace felt when she was in the strange dark forest?

## RESOURCES

<u>Parent</u>: Sometimes it is easier for children to talk to a third party about their family problems. This might be a neighbor, aunt, babysitter, or grandparent. Encourage these expressions to this other caring adult.

<u>Child</u>: Think about someone in your life whom you trust and feel close to and ask them if he or she would be willing to listen to you talk about your family's problems.

Do you think the Sun and Moon knew what Grace was going through?

How did Grace feel when she got back to a familiar place?

## FAMILIARITY

<u>Parent</u>: It is natural for you to get distracted during the divorce. However, remember your child's need for routine and structure actually increases during emotional times.

<u>Child</u>: Identify those people and places where you loved to go before your parents began fighting, places that were fun, happy and safe. Go there as often as you can.

Whom does the comforting hollow tree remind you of in your life?

How was Grace feeling about being alone?

## TIMING

<u>Parent</u>: Don't be alarmed if your child doesn't respond to you the way he or she used to. Realize your child's timing for his or her expressions and acceptance might be different than yours.

<u>Child</u>: It is normal for parents to go through changes during a divorce. Look for what has changed about your parents as well as what has remained the same. You may notice your parents' moods changing more than usual during this difficult time.

Why do you think Grace stayed silent and hid behind the hollow tree?

What would you wish Grace had said to the Sun and the Moon?

## EXPRESSION

<u>Parent</u>: The reflection on your face of care and hope will over time bring the child out of his or her shell. Be patient and aware of what you are communicating with your face.

<u>Child</u>: Even though you may see worry and concern on your parents' faces, realize these are one of the many ways parents show their love for you.

How did it feel for Grace to reconnect with each of her parents?

Can you give words to Grace as she played near the pool?

## DELIGHT

<u>Parent</u>: Although not your child's job, he or she will attempt to make you happy. Recognize your child's need for your attention and to please you. Your child wants you to be happy. Delight in his or her efforts.

<u>Child</u>: Find ways to give to your parents by being playful. What children do best is play. Don't forget to play. Your playfulness will be refreshing to your family's struggle.

How do you feel about Grace playing with the Sun again?

How did Grace and the Sun know what would make each other happy?

## CONNECTING

<u>Parent</u>: Your child deeply needs to feel connected to you. Join in his or her playfulness and let it bring lightness and relief to this difficult time in your life.

<u>Child</u>: Remember some of the ways that you used to play with your parent. Enjoy these again, and also look for new ways to play with each parent.

Why did Grace give something different to the Sun than she did to the Moon?

How did Grace feel about the Sun leaving and the Moon coming?

## BLAME

<u>Parent</u>: Despite your encouragement otherwise, your child will feel responsible for your problems and will want to try to fix them. Continue to remind your child that it is not his or her responsibility or fault.

<u>Child</u>: Your parents' fighting is an adult matter. You are not the cause of their problem, nor are you the solution. Realize your parents' explanations may not make sense to you because this is a problem between adults. You will understand more as you grow older.

Why do you think Grace wondered if it was her fault?

Is there someone in your life in addition to your parents to whom you can go with your important questions?

## HOPE

<u>Parent</u>: Often the underlying struggle for a child during a divorce is the feeling of powerlessness. It is important to try to restore your child's sense of power. Allow him or her to make decisions in the home where reasonable. Knowledge is powerful. Little by little, help your child to understand the divorce at his or her own level. Empower your child to form a unique relationship with the other parent. You are not competing for a relationship with your child; you will each have one. What can also be empowering for your child is to see you moving past resentment, hostility, and blame and into a civil relationship with the other parent. This can offer your child hope that life is moving forward.

<u>Child</u>: Your parent's divorce means a new beginning for them and for you. Although you did not ask for this new beginning and may not have even wanted it, it is an opportunity for you. The opportunity is for you to create unique and separate relationships with each of your parents. Find what you like to do with each of them and notice how these can be very different. You did not have power in deciding about the divorce, but you do have power in helping to create a unique and special relationship with each parent.

How do you imagine Grace felt when she saw the Sun and the Moon meeting in the sky?

What do you hope happens as Grace grows up?